ALWAYS

KINCAID BROTHERS SERIES PREQUEL

NEW YORK TIMES BESTSELLING AUTHOR

KAYLEE RYAN

Cover Design: Book Cover Boutique
Photographer: Wander Aguiar
Editing: Hot Tree Editing
Proofreading: Deaton Author Services
Paperback Formatting: Integrity Formatting

Stay
ALWAYS
KINCAID BROTHERS SERIES PREQUEL

NEW YORK TIMES BESTSELLING AUTHOR
KAYLEE RYAN

Prologue

ORRIN

THERE IS SOMETHING TO BE said about family traditions. Especially in the Kincaid family. We take our traditions very seriously. This one, however, is one I never miss. Once a year, my dad takes my eight brothers and me—yes, you read that right. I have eight brothers—camping and fishing for an extended weekend. We leave my mom, who is also the only female in our house, on her own to do... well, whatever it is women do when they have the house to themselves. We take to the country and live our best lives. We don't worry about saying "excuse me" when we pass gas or belch, and we don't have to worry about Mom asking us if we washed behind our ears.

Yes, you read that right too. I'm not sure if you know this, but boys... guys are dirty. Especially teenage boys, prepubescent boys, and toddlers. There are nine of us, all stair-stepped in age by two years, and only one set of twins. The babies, Maverick and Merrick.

I'm ranked first in the lineup. Beneath me, we have Declan, Brooks, Sterling, Rushton, Archer, Ryder, and then the twins. It goes without saying there has never been a dull moment growing up in our house. My brothers might drive me crazy, but I'd lay my life down for them.

"Boys," Dad says, and we all stop what we're doing and gather around the campfire. We all know what's coming. The same speech he gives us every single year. "Don't ever expect anything in this life to be handed to you. You have to work hard and love even harder."

"You work hard every day building things, right, Daddy?" six-year-old Maverick asks.

"That's right."

"And you love Momma hard?" Merrick, his twin, asks.

My brothers and I snicker at that, and even Dad cracks a smile. "With every breath," he tells him.

My dad lets his eyes fall on each of us. "I love you, boys. Know that you can always come to me with anything. Me or your mother. We're here for you always."

A chorus of "We know" and "love you too" rings out around the fire.

"Flashlight tag!" Archer cheers, and everyone scurries to their tents to grab their flashlights.

No matter how old we get, we're never too old for a game of flashlight tag with our brothers.

Chapter 1

ORRIN

I CAN'T TAKE MY EYES off her. I've been watching her all night, but that's nothing new. Every single time Jade Sanders is anywhere near, my eyes stay glued to her. Of course, I try to do it on the sly. I don't need my brothers giving me shit, but truthfully, if it got me the girl, I wouldn't even care what they had to say. They can dish it out all day long if she's mine.

"See something you like?" Declan asks.

"Just wondering when Deacon's going to do this thing."

"Uh-huh." He laughs. "I'm sure that's why

you're staring at that table full of beautiful women that our baby cousin is currently sitting with.

"I plead the fifth." I grin, and so does he.

"Just ask her out already. Anytime she's around, your eyes follow her. It doesn't matter where she is in the room."

I think about denying it, but there's no point. My brothers and I are close, all nine of us, even the twins who are the babies of the family. "Can't help it."

"Just go talk to her."

"Thought about it," I confess.

"And what's stopping you?"

"Been a long time since I asked a woman out on a date."

He nods. "I get that, man, trust me, single dad here, remember?" He points to his chest. "She and Ramsey have gotten close. Hell, those four are thick as thieves." He motions toward the booth where Ramsey, our baby cousin, her best friend, Palmer, Palmer's sister, Piper, and Jade, who is Piper's best friend, are sitting. They're all laughing and talking, and they keep glancing this way.

"Just like riding a bike," Declan says, slapping a hand on my shoulder.

"Then why haven't you done it?"

"You know my situation is different. Besides, I have a sassy little girl who I spend all my free time with."

"You're a great dad, Dec. You can take time for yourself."

He nods. "Yeah, but I want to give it all to her." A smile comes over his face. "I still remember the day Cassie came to the shop asking if we could talk. I assumed it was like any other hookup, you know? She wanted to get together again, but I was going to politely decline. I was scared as hell that day, O. I thought my life was over. I was having a baby with a woman I'd met once. Then I heard my girl's first cries, held her in my arms, and it changed me. I know it sounds crazy, brother, but that's what happened. I'd give my daughter all my days and all my minutes over a random hookup."

"What's going on over here?" Sterling turns from where he was talking to my best friend, Deacon.

"Just giving Orrin a pep talk," I tell our brother.

"Should I go get Dad?" Sterling jokes.

"Fuck off," I grumble, and my brothers both grin.

Speaking of my best friend, I catch his eyes from just a few feet away, and he gives me a nod. I grin, knowing what's about to go down. "It's time," I tell Declan and Sterling. We break up, making sure to let everyone quietly know that it's showtime.

I watch as Deacon pulls Ramsey to the small stage. It's as if they're not in a room full of friends and family as they stare into each other's eyes. When Deacon drops to one knee, the room goes crazy. He hasn't asked yet, but we all know it's just a formality. Those two are the real deal.

Ramsey nods, and they're kissing. I smile as my eyes stray to where Jade's sitting. She's smiling as she wipes her eyes. Deacon's sisters, Piper and Palmer, stand and hug one another. Jade slides out of the booth, and instead of heading to congratulate the happy couple like her friends, she slips out the door.

My feet are moving before I can think better of it. I have plenty of time to let the crowd around the happy couple die down before giving them my personal congratulations. Right now, I have an auburn-haired beauty to check on.

When I push open the door, the warm Georgia air hits me. I scan my surroundings until I find her. She's sitting on a picnic table underneath a Willow Tree off to the side of the Tavern. I know from when Ramsey worked here that it's a popular spot for the employees to take their breaks and even patrons to get some fresh air. Her long auburn hair blows in the gentle breeze, making me wish I could reach out and run my fingers through the silky strands.

Shoving my hands into the pocket of my jeans, I make my way toward her. She looks up as I approach and quickly wipes at her eyes. All good intentions to not touch her fly out the window. I crouch down so we're eye to eye and push her gorgeous auburn hair out of her eyes. "What's going on? Who do I need to give a beat down?" I ask, and her wide smile has my heart squeezing in my chest.

"No one." She smiles with watery eyes. "I'm just being silly."

"Tell me about it."

She looks down to her lap, where she twines her hands together.

Reaching out, I place my index finger under her chin so I can capture her gaze. "I'm a good listener. I have eight brothers, and I'm the oldest. This isn't my first rodeo," I tease, trying to get another smile out of her, and it works.

"I'm just happy for them."

I nod. "They're good together."

"They really are."

"What else?" I can see in her eyes she's holding something back.

"What do you mean?"

"Tell me what else you're thinking, sweetheart." Her mouth opens as if she's going to tell me what it is that's plaguing her, but she quickly closes it. "Jade?"

"I can't tell you."

"Of course you can."

She shakes her head. "No. It's too embarrassing."

"Did you forget that part where I grew up with eight brothers? Eight," I repeat, making her smile. "There is nothing that could come out of that pretty mouth of yours that could embarrass me. Trust me on this."

She gives me a soft chuckle as a reward, and my heart races just a little faster at the sound. "Fine." She rolls her eyes playfully, huffing out a breath. "I'm a little bit envious."

I nod. "Yeah. They've got something special. That's nothing to be embarrassed about."

She covers her face with her hands and groans. "I can't believe I just told you that. I'm mortified."

Reaching up, I gently pull her hands from her face. "There is nothing wrong with being envious."

"Maybe not, but I should never have told you that."

"Will it make you feel better if I confess something too?"

She tilts her head to the side to study me. "Is it as equally embarrassing?" There's a slight roll of her lips that tells me while she might be embarrassed about her confession, she's enjoying teasing me all the same.

"Do you want it to be?"

"Yes." She nods, flashing me a grin.

"How about this? How about I give you two for your one?"

"Now we're talking." She sits up straighter, and while her eyes are still glassy from her earlier tears, dampness is no longer coating her cheeks.

"I'm envious of them too."

"Come on, Orrin. I thought you'd take this seriously." She smacks lightly at my arm. Before she can remove her hand, I take it in mine.

"I am taking this seriously. I'm telling you the truth."

She studies me for several heartbeats. "Fine. Where's my number two confession?" I can't tell if she really does believe me or if she wants to hear my second truth before she passes her official judgment.

"Number two." I stroke my thumb over her knuckles while staring into her eyes. "I've wanted to ask you out for a long time." My heart is hammering so hard in my chest that I worry that she can hear it. My palms are sweaty, but that's not reason enough for me to drop her hand. Her skin is so damn soft. I'm not ready to give that up. Not yet.

Her mouth opens and quickly closes. Then she starts to laugh. "Come on." She shakes her head. "I'm being real with you, and you're toying with me."

"Jade?" I wait for her laughter to subside and for her to give me her full attention. "You really know how to smash a man's ego." I smile softly. "I'm being more real with you than I've been in a damn long time where women are concerned. In fact, I'll prove it." I tuck a loose strand of hair behind her ear. "Have dinner with me."

"Wait. For real?" There's disbelief in her tone and what looks a lot like hope in her eyes.

"For real," I assure her.

I expect her to argue some more, and I'm prepared to do whatever it is I need to do in order to convince her that I'm being truthful. However, the auburn-haired beauty surprises me with a whispered, "Yes."

"Yeah?" I can't contain my smile. "Wait. Don't answer that. I'm not giving you a chance to change your mind." She giggles, and I want to bottle the sound. "Tonight?"

"Well, we're all kind of here for Ramsey and Deacon. It would be rude to leave for a date or dinner, I mean."

"Oh, no, it's a date, sweetheart." Her cheeks flush, and I've never wanted to kiss someone so badly in my entire life.

"Tomorrow?"

"It's Sunday."

"And?"

"Sure. Tell me when and where."

This time I'm the one to laugh. "That's not how this is going to work. How am I supposed to get you to fall in love with me if I don't woo you?"

"Woo me?"

"Yes. I'll be at your place at five. I know we both have to work the next day, so we won't stay out late. Not this time."

"This time?"

I smile. "This first of many." Not able to help myself, I lean in and press my lips to her cheek. "Come on. We have a happy couple to congratulate." I stand and offer her my hand. She places hers in mine, and it feels right, just like I knew it would. I hold her hand all the way to the door, then drop it, placing mine on the small of her back, leading her back into the Tavern.

Chapter 2

JADE

MY BEDROOM LOOKS LIKE A clothing tornado just blew through. I've changed no less than ten times, and I'm still standing here in my new matching bra and panty set, not sure what I'm going to wear to dinner tonight with Orrin.

I went shopping earlier and bought my new lingerie, and even a new sundress, but now that I'm home, I don't want to wear it. I can't ever remember a time when I've been this nervous about a date. Orrin is a few years older than me. As Deacon's best friend and me being Piper's best friend, we saw a lot of each other. He was a crush, but nothing more. I went away to college and forgot about him.

However, since I've been home, every time I'm around him, I can't seem to see anyone else. He's aged well. Hell, he and his brothers and even Deacon, Piper's brother, could all be models. I mean, if I were to see them modeling their undies, I'd buy that magazine. Trust me. You would too.

My phone rings, and I stare down at the screen. It's Piper. I haven't told her about my date, and the guilt weighs heavy on me. With a sigh, I grab the device and swipe at the screen. "Hey."

"Hi. What are you doing tonight? Heath's working. I thought we could grab dinner."

"Oh, uh, I would, but I have plans."

"Plans?"

"Yep."

"No biggie. What are you doing?"

"Going to dinner."

"With who?" She chuckles. "Is this top secret or something? What's going on with you? You sound funny, and you're being evasive."

"Orrin."

"What about Orrin?"

"I'm having dinner with Orrin."

"What?" she screeches. "When did this happen? Why am I just now finding out about this? Wait, yesterday, you said Orrin was your pick. Did you make a move? Damn, I'm proud of you," Piper rattles on.

"He asked me. It happened yesterday at the Tavern."

"What? How in the hell did I miss that?"

"I walked outside for some air right after the proposal. Orrin followed me."

"So, he asked you to dinner?"

"Yep."

"Where is he taking you?"

"I don't know." I move to the corner of my room and sit on the small chair. "I don't know where he's taking me, and I don't know what to wear. I've tried on ten outfits, and none of them are right. I'm kind of freaking out here, Pipes."

"Take a deep breath. Orrin is a great guy."

"I know that. I still want to look good for him."

"You need to just be you, Jade. Don't try to be someone you think he wants you to be. Be you, and that's the *you* he asked out. Remember that."

"I know."

"It's dinner. Go with a sundress or some dressier shorts, and you'll be fine."

"I bought a new sundress today."

"Perfect."

"I don't know."

"Just message him and ask him what you need to wear."

"I don't have his number. He said he would pick me up at five. I just assumed since Willow River is such a small town, he knew where I lived."

"I'm sure he does, and if not, he has ways to find out. Like you said, this is Willow River."

"I really like him, Pipes. At least what I know of him since I've been back in town." I've never admitted that before, because I always thought the chances of Orrin and I getting together were slim to none. Now, things have changed, and I'm kind of freaking out.

"Okay. We're going to hang up, and I'm going to call you back with a video chat. We're going to figure this out."

"Thank you." I hit End, and a few seconds later, my phone rings again, this time with a video call. "Hey." I smile.

"Oh, love the hair. Those loose curls are perfect."

"Thanks. Okay, here's what I have so far." I switch the camera to the bed and show her the mounds of clothes that I'm going to be cursing myself for later when I have to hang them all back up in my closet.

"What's that green? Is that a dress?" Piper asks.

I reach down and pick up the emerald green dress I bought for tonight. "Yes. This is the one I bought today."

"Wear that. Do you still have those strappy black sandals?"

"Yes."

"Those too. Put them on. I'll wait."

"Fine." I laugh. I turn the camera back around and place it on the nightstand.

"Damn, did you buy that set today, too?" she asks.

I look down at the dark emerald bra and panties. "Yes. It was a splurge. Not that I think we're going to get to a point in the night that Orrin will see them, but they make me feel sexy."

"Because they're hot as fuck," Piper says. "And it's always best to be prepared for these kinds of things. You never know where the night might lead, and there is nothing wrong with you making the choice to show this little get-up to your man."

"He's not my man."

"Oh, he's your man," she assures me. "I saw the way he couldn't keep his eyes off you."

"Stop. You're going to get my hopes up and make the butterflies in my belly worse. I'm already nervous as hell."

"It's just Orrin."

"Right." I pull the sundress over my head. "Okay. What do you think?" I twirl so she can see me.

"I think you look beautiful, Jade. Truly. Orrin is going to swallow his tongue when he sees you."

"You think so?"

"Yes. Take a deep breath. Tonight is going to be great. I have a good feeling about this."

"I'm trying not to get too excited."

"Why the hell not?"

"I don't know. I guess I don't want to get my hopes up. One date doesn't mean forever."

"No, but that's how forever starts. It's okay to let yourself be excited. If it doesn't work out, then it doesn't work out. But you can't hold back and not put yourself out there. You'll regret it."

"You're right."

"Wait, can you say that again? I need to hit Screen Record."

"Ha ha." I shake my head and pick the phone up from the nightstand. "It's been a really long time since a date excited me this much. I know I need to stop letting my nerves get the best of me."

"Yes. Do that. And have fun. Call me later, or you know, tomorrow." She wags her eyebrows.

"I'll call you tonight when I get in. I need to go. He's supposed to be here in ten minutes. I still have to find my shoes."

"Okay. Have fun." The screen goes black. Oddly I feel calmer than before. It's not that I needed Piper's validation on my outfit, but not doing it alone helped ease some of my anxiety about tonight.

Tossing my phone on the bed, I rush to my closet to find the strappy sandals that Piper suggested I wear. I find them on the bottom of my shoe rack just as there's a knock at the door.

"Shit." Sandals in hand, I rush to the front door of my small two-bedroom rental. With my hand on the knob, I take a full deep breath before pulling open the door. Orrin smiles and waves.

"Wow," he says, letting his eyes roam over me from head to toe. I stand still, letting him take his fill. I was worried, but the look in his eyes tells me that Piper was right. Orrin wants to be here. "You're breathtaking," he says, reaching for my hand that's not holding my sandals and bringing it to his lips. "Are you ready to go?"

"Almost. I need to put these on and grab my purse. Is this okay?" I look down at my sundress. "I wasn't sure where we were going."

"It's perfect."

I nod and bite down on my cheek to keep from

smiling. "Come in. I'll just be a minute." I step back, letting him pass, before closing the door and moving to the couch. I sit and begin to wrangle on my damn strappy sandals. They're cute as hell but a pain in the ass to put on.

"Let me." Before I know what's happening, Orrin sits next to me on the couch and pulls my legs into his lap. With deft fingers, he manages to assemble my sandals better and faster than I ever have. He runs his calloused hands up my calf before clearing his throat and moving his hand back to my ankles. "Ready?"

"Y-Yes. Let me grab my purse." My knees tremble as I stand. Orrin's there, his hands on my hips, smiling up at me. "Thank you," I tell him, feeling my face flush.

He nods, and I move to the kitchen to grab my purse and phone and make sure I have my wallet before moving back to the living room. "All set?"

I nod and smile, not able to find my voice. He places his hand on the small of my back and leads me out to the front porch. I stop to make sure the door is locked and then allow him to guide me to the passenger door of his truck.

"Where are we going?" I ask him.

"It's a surprise." He gives me a smile, and my heart flutters in my chest. I'm in trouble with this one.

"You're lucky I like surprises," I tease.

"I'll have to remember that for next time. I knew this would be taking a chance, not telling you."

"A good chance," I say, smiling even though he's looking at the road. "When I was a little girl, I used to love when my parents would surprise me."

"Old boyfriends?" he asks.

"Nah, you're the first. I mean, the first guy. The first date to surprise me. Well, unless you count the guy I'd been dating for about six months my senior year of college. He surprised me when I showed up at his apartment for our date. He was in a compromising position with his best friend's girlfriend. He forgot we made plans."

"Fuck. What an asshole. I'm sorry."

I can hear the sincerity in his voice. "It's fine. I wasn't in love with him or anything. I mean, I liked him, but we'd only been dating about six months, and I was pretty focused on graduation and finals. We didn't really see each other all that often. Looking back, I now know that should have been an indicator that we weren't meant to be."

He scoffs. "He's a dumbass. If you were mine, I'd make the time."

"It was a good thing. I can see that now."

"Damn right it was. I'm sorry that he cheated on you, but if that hadn't happened, you might not be sitting in my truck, and we wouldn't be on the way to our first of what I hope is many dates."

"Many?" I can hear the surprise in my voice. "You sound like it's a sure thing."

"I can be very persuasive," he says with a chuckle. "That sounded creepy as fuck. I just mean, I want to get to know you, and I hope that you give me the chance to do that."

"Let's see how this surprise turns out," I tease.

"Oh, it's going to be good. I enrolled the help of my brothers. You're about to witness an event planned by nine Kincaids. I'm confident of our wooing skills."

My laugh bubbles out of my chest. "I can't wait to see this."

He glances over and grins. "All a part of my master plan."

"Oh, yeah?"

"Yep." His boyish grin has my belly twisting with excitement.

Chapter 3

ORRIN

I TURN ON THE ROAD, my road, and I see her shift in her seat out of the corner of my eye.

"Are we going to your house?" she asks.

"We are."

"Oh." I can hear the uncertainty in her voice.

"I promise, it's not whatever it is that you're thinking in the pretty head of yours," I tell her.

"How do you know what's in my head?" Her tone is defensive, and I know what she's thinking. She thinks I brought her here to hook up. That couldn't be farther from the truth. Sure, when that happens with us, I'd want her here in my bed, but that's not what tonight is about.

"Instinct, I guess."

"So, what are we doing here then? You asked me to dinner, and you brought me to your house. What am I supposed to think, Orrin?" She sounds upset, and that's just not going to work for me.

Pulling into my driveway, I put the truck in Park, kill the engine and turn to face her. "That's not what tonight is about, Jade. I promise you that. I wanted this night to be special. We only get one first date, and I wanted you all to myself. With my brothers' help, and that includes Deacon, this is what we came up with. I'll show you, and if you want to leave, I promise you, sweetheart, I will take you anywhere you want to go if you don't feel comfortable here." I take a deep breath, waiting for her reply.

She's quiet for way longer than my poor racing heart can take when she finally says, "Show me."

"Jade?" I wait for her to look at me. "You have my word. At any time if you want to leave, you tell me, and we'll go. No questions asked. No pressure to stay. You control this. Okay?"

She nods. "Okay."

"Wait for me." I point to where her hand is on the door handle. "When you're with me, I take care of you. That means I open your door." She sits back in her seat and drops her hand. Satisfied, I grab my keys and phone, shoving both in my pocket as I walk to her door to open it for her.

Pulling open her door, I smile and offer her my hand. She takes it and climbs out of my truck. I link our fingers together and lead her to the front door. Thanks to keyless entry, I type in my code, and the lock releases, allowing me to push open the door, and guide her inside.

"You can set your things wherever. We're going to be outside in the backyard."

"Okay." She drops her purse to the coffee table but keeps her phone in her hand.

"This way." Once again, I place my palm on the small of her back and lead her toward the patio door. "Sterling texted me when I got to your place telling me they were done."

"The anticipation is killing me," she says, smiling over at me.

Relief washes over me that she seems to feel relaxed here. I know this was a risk, but I'm hoping that it pays off. "Remember, at any point in the night, if you want to go, we can. I'm not saying that because I don't want you here. I want you to stay always, but I also want you to be comfortable."

"Thank you." She peers up at me under long lashes, and all I want to do is kiss the hell out of her.

Keeping myself in check, I open the patio door, and we step outside. It's hot but not unbearably so. As soon as the sun starts to set, it might cool down, but that's okay. I have a fan and blankets. At least I'm supposed to have them. That was Rushton's job.

"What is all of this?" Jade asks, her eyes scanning my backyard.

"Well, it's movie night. I thought about going to the theater, but I really just wanted to spend time with you. I wanted to be able to talk if we wanted to so we could get to know each other better, and I didn't feel like getting shushed at the theater all night long. So, we have our own screen and projector. That was Declan and Deacon's job."

"You gave Deacon and all of your brothers jobs for our date night?" She's shaking her head.

"Damn right I did. We did some major planning and work to pull this off tonight."

"It's perfect. Thank you, Orrin."

The smile she gives me lights up her face and sets my heart into a gallop. "You're welcome. I'm glad you're here."

"So tell me about all of this." She waves at the setup in my backyard. "Who helped with what?"

"So you already know that Declan and Deacon teamed up for the outdoor movie screen and projector. Rush was in charge of the blankets and pillows. Brooks was in charge of drinks, and we have wine, beer, and water in the cooler." I pause, letting all that sink in. "Sterling was in charge of food. We have chicken salad sandwiches, which Piper said were your favorite." I wink, and she nods, her cheeks turning pink. "Fresh fruit, chips, and chocolate chip cookies, which are homemade by me if you count opening up the pack and placing the little squares on the cookie sheet." I flash her a cheesy grin. "And I basically helped them all make sure everything was perfect. I could have done it all myself, but my brothers wanted to help, and honestly, it was nice to have them here with me." I shrug at my confession. However, it's the truth. My brothers have my back always, just like I have theirs. Them being here kept me from overthinking my choice to bring her here.

She laughs. "That definitely counts."

"That's what I told Piper. Anyway, Archer and Ryder were responsible for all the twinkle lights you see, and Maverick and Merrick were in charge of music and movie selection."

"Music and movies. Nice." She takes a few steps toward our little backyard oasis and turns to look at me. "I can't believe that you did all of this. You got your brothers and my best friend involved. This is... I don't really know what to say, Orrin."

"Say that you want to stay and have dinner with

me. Say that you'll curl up on that makeshift bed and watch a movie with me."

"This was a lot of work."

"We're only ever going to have one first date, Jade," I remind her again.

"Do you work this hard for all of your first dates?" she asks.

"No." I'm quick to shut that shit down. "No, you are the one and only that I've put this kind of effort into."

"Sounds like you're getting more resourceful in your old age," she teases.

No longer able to stand the distance between us, my feet carry me until I'm standing right in front of her. So close that the toes of our shoes are touching. Resting my hand against her cheek, I wait for her to look at me. "I'd like to think it's me knowing what I want. Whether or not that has anything to do with my age, I'm not sure. I do know that it has everything to do with you. I've never done this for anyone else because I didn't want to. Not until you."

"Thank you for doing all of this. For bringing me here. Best first date ever," she whispers. Peering at me under long lashes. She grins, telling me whatever else is coming my way is to lighten the heavy I just put on our mood. "I don't know. Thirty-two is pretty ancient," she teases.

"Just because you're still in your twenties, Miss I'm Twenty-Seven, doesn't mean I'm ancient in my thirties."

She places her hand on my chest, and I cover it with my own, holding it there. "I was just messing with you."

I bring her hand to my lips and kiss her knuckles. "I know you were. Now, come on. You can pick the music while I feed you." Holding her hand, I lead her to the thick layer of blankets and mounds of pillows that Rushton set up. I don't know where he found them all. More than likely I'm going to spend this week delivering items back to my parents and my brothers, but it's all worth it. The night has barely started, and I already know I'll have zero regrets.

"After you." I motion for her to take a seat. She drops to her knees and gets comfortable with me sitting next to her. Reaching into the smaller cooler, I pull out the sandwiches, the bag of salt and vinegar chips that are her favorite, and the bowl of mixed fresh fruit.

"I think I need to have a talk with my best friend," she says when she sees all her favorites.

"I didn't ask anything personal, and I didn't want to ask this, but I wanted tonight to be fun for you. I didn't want you to be starving to death."

"I would hardly starve to death, but I appreciate

all of this. No one has ever done something like this for me before."

"Because they're idiots, but I can't say that I'm upset about it. I like to be at the top of my game."

"Well, you're doing a great job so far."

"Thank you, my lady," I say in my best refined voice, making her laugh. Pulling my phone out of my pocket, I pull up my music app and hand it to her. "Here, I can listen to anything. Pick your favorite."

"I have so many," she says, taking the phone from my outstretched hand. "What's your favorite genre?"

"Honestly, I like almost all genres of music. I'm not much of a jazz fan or heavy metal, but the rest of it, I guess you could say I have an eclectic taste in music."

"I bet I can stump you," she challenges me.

"You think so?" I ask, easing back on the pillows holding my weight on my elbows.

"I know so."

"Let's do it." I nod toward my phone that she's holding in her hand.

"Hmm." She thinks while she taps at the screen, and a slow, steady smile pulls at her lips. "Okay. Doesn't matter if you know the artist or the name of the song, but you have to know the lyrics."

"Damn, sweetheart, that's going to be easy as hell."

She shrugs. "Don't be so sure." She taps at the screen, and music begins to flow from the speaker. I recognize the song immediately.

"'Try Missing You.' Jon Langston." I grin because I know I'm right.

"All right." She nods in approval. "Too easy. Let me try again."

When the next song plays, I burst out laughing. "'Dicked Down in Dallas.' I don't know who sings it, but I know that I can." She laughs and sings a few lines, and I can't help but join her.

"Okay, okay," she says, taking a deep breath and wiping the tears from her eyes from laughter. "I need to step up my game."

"Okay, I don't know the name of the song, but I can tell it's Metallica."

"Correct. 'Unforgiven,'" she tells me.

I nod, letting the beginning chords register in my mind. "I got it," I tell her, hearing the lyrics in my head.

"Okay. Try this one." She taps at the screen, and the music begins to play once again.

"'Edge of Seventeen,' Stevie Nicks."

"Shit, okay. Let's go again." Over the next hour,

she's not able to stump me. I know the lyrics, and sometimes the artist and sometimes the title, and even both more often than I thought that I would. "I concede to the master." She bows her head, handing me my phone.

"Told you that I was good." I grin. "Now, eat up so you can pick a movie."

"Why don't we watch while we eat?"

"Anything you want is fine with me." I hand her Declan's iPad and show her the app. "Pick whichever one you want."

"What do you feel like watching?" she asks, taking the iPad and scrolling.

"You."

"Come on, be serious."

"I am. Do you really think that I'm going to waste time watching whatever comes across that screen when I can be watching you? Not likely."

"I... I don't know what to say to that," she admits.

"You don't say anything. You pick a movie, curl up next to me, and let me watch you."

"Are you aware that makes you sound like a creeper?" She's teasing, and the tiny lift at the corner of her mouth and the sparkle in her eyes tell me so.

I shrug. "I'll own it. Pick us a movie, sweetheart."

Chapter 4

JADE

SCROLLING THROUGH THE MOVIE CHOICES, I have to bite down on my cheek to keep from smiling. This is already the best date I've ever been on. I can't believe that he went to all of this trouble and even enlisted the help of his best friend and brothers to make this night happen.

"I think we're going to go with a classic," I tell him. I tap the screen to select the movie and hand the iPad back to him.

"*Footloose.*" He chuckles. "I've seen this one so many times." I'm ready to tell him we can watch something else, but when he looks up and is wearing a devilish grin, I stop myself. "You're making it easy on me, sweetheart. I might have grown up in a house full of men, but my dad doted on my mom, and well, that means my brothers and I did as well. I've watched many chick flicks in my day."

"We can pick something else," I say, finding my words.

"Nope. This just means I can watch you all night and still discuss the movie after." He winks, and my belly swarms with butterflies.

I watch as he uses his phone to turn off the music and connects the iPad to the projector. I'm not sure how it all works, but when the opening credits of *Footloose* appear on the screen, I smile.

"I tested this at least a dozen times," he confesses. "I didn't want to get you here under the premise of dinner and a movie and not be able to deliver. This was the first thing set up today because it was the most technical."

"It's a sweet setup."

"They did great, but don't tell them that I said that." He laughs.

"You're lucky to have them."

He nods. "Yeah, they can annoy the hell out of me, but I would throw hands for them any day of the week."

"I always wanted a sibling."

"I can share mine with you," he says. His voice is soft and holds so much conviction that it makes me think his words hold a different meaning. "Eat up," he says, sliding the rest of my food my way and nodding toward the bowl of fruit between us.

My stomach is a mess of nervous excitement, but I manage to finish the rest of my sandwich, eat a few chips and a few pieces of fruit before waving the white flag. Orrin quickly cleans up, tossing everything back into the cooler.

"Beer? Wine? Water?" he asks.

"Just water, please."

He nods, pulls out a bottle of water, and wipes it off with a napkin before handing it to me.

We go back to watching the movie. Sitting outside beneath the stars, on a mountain of blankets and pillows, watching one of my favorite movies is not where I thought this night would lead, but I couldn't be happier that it did.

I shift, needing a new position, and feel his hand on my arm. I turn to look at him, and his eyes bore into mine. "Everything okay?" I ask when he continues to watch me.

"Can I hold you?" His voice is soft. So much so that if I hadn't been laser-focused on him, I might not have heard him.

There's an uncertainty in his eyes, which surprises me. I've never seen Orrin anything but 100 percent confident. "Is that what you want?" I ask, tilting my head to the side to study him. I don't know why I ask the question. It's obvious that's what he wants, or he wouldn't have asked, but something about him asking for permission settles my nerves and gives me confidence. It's a heady feeling knowing that he respects me enough to ask.

"Do I want you in my arms while you watch this movie, and I watch you? Yes. More than anything."

"Why ask for permission? Why not just make your move?"

"Because you're different, Jade. I don't want you just for tonight. I want you for always. I was afraid you would leave or ask to go home, and I want you to stay always. With me."

I swallow the lump in my throat. "We're missing the movie." I grin.

He smiles is breathtaking and lights up his face. "Come here, sweetheart." He stretches his legs out in front of him and opens them wide, patting the space between them. I don't hesitate to move and settle between his thighs. He wraps his arms around me, pulling my back to his chest. "Much better," he says, his lips next to my ear.

He rustles around, moving more of the pillows

behind his back before settling and taking me with him. "Are you comfortable?" he asks.

"Yes."

I feel his lips press to the top of my head, and his arms tighten around me. Neither one of us say another word unless it's to sing along to the soundtrack or repeat the lines of the movie. His hold on me never wavers, and those kisses on the top of my head increase as the night goes on.

When the credits roll, I sit up and turn to look at him. "Thank you for humoring me."

"It's a great movie," he says, reaching out and tucking my hair behind my ear. "You want to watch another one? Or do you want some fruit? Oh, I almost forgot." He reaches into the cooler, pulls out a container, and hands it to me. "They're chocolate chip cookies. Piper said they were your favorite."

"If I didn't know any better, I'd think you really are trying to make me fall in love with you." I'm teasing, but I can feel my cheeks heat from embarrassment.

"Would that be such a bad thing?" he asks softly.

"I can think of worse," I tease, trying to lighten the mood that I turned serious with my big mouth.

"And I can't think of anything better."

I've heard Ramsey drone on about how Deacon

makes her feel inside. How she has butterflies, and it feels as though her body melts when he says or does certain things. I've read romance novels where the authors describe the main character as swooning, but I never really understood. I thought I did. I thought I was able to comprehend the meaning, but it's not until this moment that I feel the true force of the word.

"What's next on this grand adventure?" I ask, once again moving the topic toward something that will keep me from throwing myself at him. I can't attack him with my mouth on our first date.

"We can watch another movie, or just listen to music and talk. I can just hold you while we look up at the stars, or we can go for a drive. Honestly, Jade, I don't really care what you decide to do next as long as It's not me taking you home. Not yet. I'm not ready for that yet."

"Music and talk?" I ask.

"Okay." He leans forward like he's going to kiss me, and I quickly lick my lips, but his land on my temple. Grabbing his phone, he taps at the screen, and Luke Combs fills the night air singing about forever.

"May I use your restroom?" I ask him.

"Of course. Come. I'll show you where it is." He taps my hip, and I stand, offering him my hand and pulling him to his feet. He doesn't let go as he guides me into his house and down the hall to the restroom.

"I'll be in the kitchen," he says, releasing me.

I nod and disappear behind the bathroom door. I quickly take care of business and wash my hands before staring at my reflection in the mirror. My eyes are bright with excitement, and my face is tinged pink. I think I've blushed a hundred times tonight. I guess my body just decided to stay flushed.

Taking a deep breath, I open the door, turn out the light and go in search of Orrin. I find him sitting on the kitchen island, facing away from me. I pad softly into the room. I don't stop until I'm standing in front of him. He opens his legs, and on instinct, I step between them. He wraps his arms around me in a hug, and there is nothing I can do but return his embrace.

"I like having you here. More than I could have ever thought possible."

I pull back and peer up at him. "I like being here."

"This isn't a one-time thing, right? Please tell me you'll give me another date."

"I'd like that."

He moves his hands to rest against my cheeks. "Can I kiss you?"

"Is that what you want?" I repeat our earlier words.

He grins. "Yes."

"This is our first date." I feel his hands start to drop, so I quickly grip his wrists, holding them in place. "This *is* our first date, but it doesn't feel that way. It feels like we've been here before."

He nods. "I thought maybe it was just me."

"It's not just you. I feel... connected to you." My words are soft as I wait for him to look at me like I've lost my damn mind. The look never comes.

"It feels right, Jade. We feel right. I don't want this to be our only date. Hell, I don't want to take you home. I'd love nothing more than to carry you to my room and wrap you up in my arms and hold you all night long."

"Just hold me?" I ask. I can't believe I'm being this bold that I feel comfortable enough with him to speak my mind.

"If that's your subtle way of asking me if I'd make love to you, then I'll have to revert that answer back to you. But first, I want you to know that it would be an honor for you to give me that kind of trust, to allow me inside you. It would also be an honor to be the man you chose to sleep next to. To know that you feel safe enough to let me hold you all night long in my bed. I want it all, Jade. I want anything and everything you're ready to give me."

"I want all of that, but I have to be up early tomorrow. I... don't want to rush that."

He grins. "When I make love to you, I'm going to need hours. Maybe even days," he says, leaning in and softly brushing his lips with mine. "Let's go back outside. We can talk a little more, and when you're ready, I'll take you home."

"Orrin, tonight has been incredible. I've loved every minute. Please thank your brothers and Deacon for me for helping you set this all up."

"Nope. Not until I know you're mine. If they find out how damn sweet you are, they might try and steal you from me. I'm not going to let that happen."

"Stop." I laugh, stepping out of his reach. "You and I both know that the bro code between the nine of you is strong, and Deacon, he doesn't see anyone but Ramsey."

"Like I can't see anyone but you."

I pull in a deep breath. "Did you spend last night and today thinking about things you could say to me to make me feel as though my insides are melting into a puddle of goo?"

He laughs. "No, sweetheart. I spent the day helping each of my brothers, making sure everything was perfect for tonight. As far as the things I say, I'm just speaking from my heart. I'm not holding back with you. For the first time in my life, I've found someone who makes me want more, and I can't believe I'm going to say this, but I'm taking my old man's lecture I've heard a thousand times by heart."

"And what's that?"

"Work hard and love harder."

My mouth falls open.

"I'm not saying I'm in love with you." He hops off the counter and steps in close. He wraps his arms around me but leaves us enough distance that we can still look into each other's eyes. "But for the first time in my life, I feel myself falling. I know it's fast, but I've wanted to ask you out for months."

"Is that the Kincaid family motto?"

He chuckles. "Something like that. Our dad, he passes out words of wisdom like its candy, but that one, that's the one he always comes back to time and time again."

"He gives good advice."

"He does. Come on, let's head back outside." Stepping away, he takes my hand and leads me outside. Once we're on the patio, I know I need to swallow my nerves and address his confession.

"Hey, Orrin." He stops and turns to look at me, giving me his full attention. "I can feel myself falling too."

I don't know what I was expecting, but it wasn't for him to turn, lift me in his arms and kiss the breath from my lungs. His hands grip the back of my thigh, as he kisses me like this could be his last chance to ever do so. When he finally pulls away, he rests his forehead against mine. Neither one of us say a word as we try to catch our breath. I don't know how much time passes before he begins walking, carrying me to the blanket. He sets me on my feet and drops down to the blanket. I follow suit, and he pulls me into his arms. Together we stare up at the night sky, not needing words to fill the silence.

This is, without a doubt, the best first date I've ever been on.

"I hope it's our last," he says huskily.

I freeze, not realizing I said the words out loud, making his chest shake with silent laughter. "It's my best first date too. Not because of what we did, but because it was you." He kisses the top of my head, and I know I'm in deep trouble with this one.

Chapter 5

ORRIN

FOR OVER A MONTH, JADE and I have been dating, and I feel as though the smile on my face is now permanently etched there. If we're not working, we're together. My place, her place, dinner, it doesn't matter as long as I get to see her and kiss her every single day.

I never imagined myself falling in love. Not really. I always knew I wanted to get married and have a family one day. I grew up in a house of crazy brothers, watching my parents love one another with everything inside them. I wanted that. I just didn't think much about getting there or what it would look like for me. Now I know.

It looks like Jade.

After that night at my house, I knew in my bones that she was the one for me, so I decided to take things slow, at least where sex is concerned. I wanted her to know that I'm with her because of the person that she is, not for the sole purpose of getting off. There has been a lot of kissing and exploring each other's bodies, but I always stop us before we get to the finale. Well, not the finale, really. My girl always gets hers, and she takes care of me too, but I've yet to make love to her. It's been a struggle holding back, one I'm ready to end.

Tonight.

It's Sunday evening, and Mom's been hounding me about bringing Jade to dinner. I've held off, not wanting to scare her, but last night we went to the Tavern, and Ramsey took the decision out of my hands. She asked Jade if she'd see her at Sunday dinner. I played it off like I forgot to mention it. Jade smiled and easily agreed. I could see the question in her eyes as to if I really wanted her to go, but she accepted the invite anyway.

It's not that I didn't want to take her to dinner or that I didn't want her to meet my family. Hell, she's already met all of them. I did, however, want to take her to Sunday dinner as my girlfriend. Not just as some girl I've been dating. She's more than that to me, and taking someone home and to Sunday dinner is a big damn deal. So big, in fact, that none of us have ever done it. Not even my niece, Blakely's mom, made the cut. That's a story for another day.

So, my little cousin has me showing my hand sooner than I intended. Not because I'm not certain that Jade is the woman for me, but because I was giving her time. I've known since that first night but knew that it made me sound crazy. I wanted to give her a few months to come to my way of thinking, but the time is now. I won't take her home without knowing she's mine. Maybe it's irrational, but it's important to me.

That means today is the day. I have a plan, it's corny as hell, but it fits us. Grabbing my phone, I climb out of my truck and make my way to her front door. It opens before I even get a chance to knock, and behind it is Jade. Her long red hair is hanging over her shoulders. She's wearing a flannel shirt over what looks like a tank top and a pair of cutoffs. She takes my damn breath away. All I can do is stand there and take in her beauty.

"Orrin?"

"I love you." The words fly out of my mouth without caution.

Her eyes grow wide with shock. "You love me?" she asks slowly.

"Shit."

"It's fine, a slip of the tongue." She's quick to let me off the hook.

"Can I come in?"

"Sure." She steps back and allows me into her home. As soon as the door closes, I swoop her up in my arms and carry her to the couch. I sit with her still in my arms and hold her close. "I'm sorry, Jade. That's not how I wanted to tell you. I had this big plan, but I ruined it."

"It's fine, Orrin."

"It's not fine." I pull back so she can see my eyes. "When you opened the door, you took my breath away. All I could think about is how much you mean to me. It's not that I didn't mean the words, Jade. I do love you. I just wanted to be a little more romantic about it. A little more us."

"A little more us? Orrin, we are us. Are you feeling all right?" Her tone is lighter, which tells me that she's teasing, trying to lighten the moment. She does that a lot, but it's not going to work this time. It's time for all my real, and it's about to be unleashed on her.

Keeping her on my lap, I manage to dig in my pocket for my phone. Pulling up my playlist, I hit Play, and Jet's "Are You Gonna Be My Girl" begins to play.

Jade tosses her head back in laughter. "Are you asking me to be your girl, Orrin Kincaid?"

"Yes. All mine. No one else, just me. Forever."

"Forever is a long time."

"Not nearly long enough." I close the distance between us and press my lips to hers. "Jade Sanders, will you be my girl?"

"I don't know. I'm kind of seeing this guy. He's sexy as hell and owns his own body shop. He's kind of important to me."

"Yeah?" I don't bother to hide my grin.

"Uh-huh, I'd go as far as saying that I'm in love with him. I've just been too nervous to say it first."

"I need to hear you say it," I tell her. "I need those three words from these lips."

She moves to straddle my hips, resting her hands on my shoulders. I grip her hips, holding her to me. "I love you."

"Thank fuck." My lips crash with hers and call me crazy, but this feels different. Knowing that she loves me and that she finally knows that I love her, our kiss feels like... more. I kiss her like it's the first time and the last time. I never want to stop kissing her. Eventually, I do pull away so we can both catch our breath.

"There's something else that I need to tell you."

"I'm listening."

"It's not that I didn't ever want to invite you to Sunday dinner. I didn't want you there until I knew you were mine. It's a sacred event in our family, and well, it was important to me that we were solid. That you loved me as much as I love you before I brought you there."

"I don't have to go. If you're not ready, I don't have to go," she repeats.

"Baby, I was ready to take you after our first date." Her eyes widen. "I know it was fast, but I fell hard. I was just waiting for you to catch up."

"I think we've been reading the same book, Orrin. I wanted to tell you so many times, but I didn't want to scare you away."

"We're a pair, huh?" I ask, pulling her into my chest. "How about from now on, we agree that even if we're scared, we say what we're feeling, what we're thinking. It's important for our future to keep the lines of communication open."

"Our future?"

"Yeah, I mean, what if our son or daughter asks to go somewhere and you say no, but I say yes. That puts us working against each other. We need to talk about these things so we can be a united front."

"Our son or daughter?" she parrots.

"Or all girls, or all boys, I don't care, really. I'm speaking hypothetically here."

"About our future children?"

"Yes. Catch up, baby. I'm saying we need to be on the same page from here on out. I could have told you weeks ago what you mean to me, and we could have been having dinner with my family all along. Instead, I've endured not spending Sunday nights with you and listening to my mom ask when I was going to bring you with me, and my brothers giving me shit, thinking it was because you didn't want to be there with me."

"Orrin, surely you knew better than that."

"I did, but it still pissed me off, which was their plan."

"You all really like to razz on each other, huh?"

"Yes, but no one else is allowed to. Well, you can, and Ramsey, of course, and I guess Deacon by association. I mean, they are getting married now."

"I love you. I love you and your big loving family."

"I love you too. Speaking of my family, we should get going. We're going to be late." I kiss her one more time before she stands from my lap.

I wait for her to grab her purse and phone and follow her out the door to my truck. "Are you nervous?" I ask, glancing over once we're on the road to see her wringing her hands together.

"What should I expect?"

"Lots of loud laughter, ribbing from my

brothers, a crushing hug from my mom and my dad, and lots of good food. I think Dad's grilling burgers."

"Orrin! I forgot the cookies that I made. We have to go back. I can't go to your parents for dinner empty-handed."

"It's fine. I told you that you don't have to bring anything. Just you." I reach over and give her leg a gentle squeeze.

"Please?"

Smiling, I turn on my signal, pull into a driveway, and turn back around. There isn't much she could ask of me that I wouldn't give her if it were within my power. "You're setting the bar high," I tell her.

"What do you mean?" she asks as we pull back into her driveway.

"My brothers, the women they bring home when they find their own Jade, they're going to have big shoes to fill." Leaning over the console, I kiss her. "Go grab your cookies, sweetheart."

She runs up the front steps, unlocks the door, and is right back outside with a clear container with a red lid in her hands. She makes sure the door is locked before she jogs back to the truck. Opening the door, she hands me the container and takes her seat next to mine.

"Hey." She smacks my hand when I reach into the container for a small sample. "Those are for your family."

"I'm your boyfriend. Do I not get to eat my girl's cookie?" I grin and wag my eyebrows.

"No, you do not, and if you don't listen, you might not ever get my er... other cookie either."

I immediately drop the cookie back into the container and shove the lid back on. Jade's laughter fills the cab of my truck. I hand her the container and put the truck in Reverse. I can wait until after dinner. Nothing is worth her cutting me off before I've had the chance to taste her everything.

Chapter 6

JADE

I TRY TO HIDE MY nerves as Orrin, with his hand locked tight around mine, leads us into the house. I have my container of cookies in my other hand, clutching them to my chest. I'm scared to death that I'm going to drop them.

This isn't my first time being at his parents' place. I've been here several times with the girls, but this is my first time as his girlfriend, and it feels different. I know his brothers, hell, I know his parents. It's not like I'm walking into a room of strangers, but it still has my belly in knots and my palms sweating. Hence the reason I'm clutching the cookies to my chest and cutting off the circulation in Orrin's hand from my tight grip. I don't want either of them to slip out of reach.

"Breathe, sweetheart," Orrin whispers in my ear. "It's just my family. You know them. They know you. It's all going to be fine." With that, he stands back to his full height and leads me inside.

As soon as we open the door, we're greeted with boisterous laughter, and I start to feel my body relax. These are people I know. They know that we've been dating. This isn't a big deal. At least, that's what I try to convince myself. Two hours ago, was fine coming here for dinner. When Orrin showed up at my door and told me he loved me, that changed everything.

I knew that I loved him, but him loving me back? That's a game changer. I'm not just some girl he's been dating. He said forever. That's one word, seven letters that change the course of both of our lives. It hasn't even been two months since our first date, and he's dropping those seven letters like they're written in stone. I'm good with it. It's crazy and fast, but when you know, you know.

Orrin and I are solid. It's his family I'm not sure about. Do they know what we just confessed to one another? How do they feel about this whirlwind relationship we're both jumping into feet first?

"Finally!" I hear a female voice call out.

Orrin laughs from beside me as his mom appears in front of us. "Jade, I'm so sorry my oldest son was keeping you from us. I'm glad he finally came to his senses." I'm shocked when she leans in and hugs me tight. "I'm so glad that you're here. I'm outnumbered. Ramsey and Blakely are not enough to balance out this crazy brood of mine," she says, releasing me from her hug.

"Thank you for having me," I say, finding my voice. I shove the container toward her. "I made cookies."

"Cookie?" I hear from behind me. I don't have time to see which brother it is because he's suddenly next to me, tossing his arm over my shoulder. "I like cookies," Archer says, grinning.

"Hands off my girl," Orrin says, picking Archer's arm up from my shoulders and letting it drop.

"Cookies?" Rushton says, pushing Archer forward, and he too drops his arm over my shoulder.

"Fuck off," Orrin grumbles. When he reaches for Rushton, his brother is faster. Rushton pulls me into his chest, wrapping his arms around me.

"No way, bro. She bakes. I'm calling dibs." Rushton smiles down at me. "It's a match made in heaven."

"I think we should let her choose," Sterling calls out. "I mean, there are nine of us." He shrugs his shoulders like it's the most logical reasoning that there's a choice.

"Oh, I like the way you think." Brooks nods. "Maybe draw straws," he suggests with a wicked grin.

"I vote for pulling names out of a hat," Ryder chimes in. "Mom, do you still have the old hat we used to use?" he asks Carol, their mom.

"The choice is obvious," Maverick says. He glances over at his twin, who grins as they have some sort of silent conversation.

"Two for one." Merrick winks at me.

"Stop!" Orrin yells.

"Now you've done it. Blake, why don't you come with me. We need to check on Papaw and the grill," Declan tells his daughter.

"I'm a good checker." She takes Declan's hand, and they step out of the room.

"Is that your vein popping?" Deacon asks with a chuckle.

"Hush." Ramsey smacks at his chest. "Jade, I'm sorry for these idiots."

"It's fine," I tell her, trying to hide my laugh because Orrin really does look like he's ready to explode.

"Rushton," Orrin growls. "Get your hands off my girlfriend. Now."

"Did you say girlfriend?" another male voice asks. We all turn to see Raymond, their dad, standing with an aluminum pan full of grilled burgers.

"Yep." Orrin is now grinning.

"Boys, leave your sister alone," Raymond tells them. "Don't rile him up. One day it's going to be you, and girlfriend or wife be damned, he will find a way to pay you back."

I am about swallow my tongue when he says wife, but I don't have time to finish the task because Orrin grabs my arm, pulling me into his chest. He wraps his arms around me protectively, and I melt into him. I feel his lips press to the top of my head, and normally I'd blush, but after that initiation, I'm just happy to be in his arms and to know he's no longer on the verge of a stroke.

"Dad, you're always taking away our fun," Maverick grumbles.

Raymond fights a grin. "You two"—he points to the twins—"I'm watching you."

"What?" Merrick scoffs. "Why are we always the ones that get blamed?"

"Double trouble," the entire room mutters, and then they all crack up laughing.

"Come and get it!" Carol calls out from what I'm assuming is the kitchen.

HOME OF THE KINCAID BROTHERS

Everyone filters out of the room, except for Orrin and me. "I'm sorry," he says as soon as it's just us.

Tilting my head back, I smile up at him. "Why are you apologizing?"

"They mean well, but they love to rile me up," he grumbles.

"Orrin, it's fine. They're your brothers. They do it because they love you. I'm fine. It actually helped to calm my nerves."

He studies me, looking for what I'm not sure, but when he sighs, letting his guard down, I know he's accepted my words as truth. "I love you." He leans down and kisses me.

"Daddy!" Blakely yells. "Uncle Orrin is giving Jade cooties." The little tattletale giggles and rushes back into the kitchen.

"I wonder which one of my brothers sent her out here?" Orrin asks.

"It doesn't matter. She's adorable, and we came here to eat with your family. We should probably do that." I start to pull away, but something his dad said stops me. "Orrin, your dad referred to me as your brothers' sister. Did I hear that right?"

This time his smile is huge and lights up his entire face. "You heard him."

"I don't understand."

"They know I would have never brought you here unless I was in love with you. That's his way of welcoming you to the family."

"Wow. This is all happening fast." I try to process his words. Orrin- this day is more than I ever could have hoped for. To have the blessing of not only his brothers, but his parents has me falling a little in love with all of them too.

"We can slow down, just don't pull away," he says, suddenly serious.

"I don't want to slow down." I go up on my toes and kiss him softly. "We could go a little faster," I tell him.

His eyes widen, and his hands tighten on my waist. "We're leaving," he says. His voice is suddenly deep and husky.

"No." I laugh. "We are having dinner with your family. We can go faster when we get home."

"Home." He nods and kisses me. "One of these days, the meaning of that word is going to mean the same for both of us."

"You're already my home, Orrin."

"Let me rephrase that. One of these days, our addresses are going to match."

Somehow, I manage to contain the giddiness that bubbles inside of me at with his confession. "Come on, boyfriend, let's eat." I step away, but he grabs my hand, and we enter the kitchen together as a united front. I catch Ramsey's eye as she makes her plate, and she grins and nods.

Everyone else acts as though I've been here a million times as Orrin's girlfriend. We all make our plates and everyone spreads out around the open area finding a seat. They have a huge kitchen table, but not enough room for all of us. The house is an open concept, so it doesn't matter if you sit at the table in the living room or on the island. It still feels as though everyone is eating together.

The rest of the evening goes off without a hitch. We eat, laugh, and end up in an intense euchre tournament of sorts. There is no more teasing, but I think that has more to do with the fact that Orrin hasn't let me out of his sight, and he's always touching me. So much so that when it's his turn to play, and I'm sitting out from a loss with my partner, which was Ramsey, he pulls a chair up beside him and has me sit next to him. Not that I mind. I want to be next to him too. I hope that I never lose that want or need to be with him.

By the time we say our goodbyes and head back to my place, it's almost ten, and I have to be up early for work tomorrow. Orrin holds my hand all the way and walks me to my door. "You should pack a bag and come stay with me," he says, standing on my front porch.

"I'm already home, and it's late."

"Yeah." He sighs. "Family dinner, take my time with you. I'm not a fan," he grumbles.

"Come on now. Tonight was fun."

"Anytime I spend with you is fun."

"Silver tongue," I say, kissing under his chin.

"Next weekend, we're staying at my place. All weekend. Friday at five, you're mine. Pack a bag and come straight from work. We're blocking out the world."

"Deal."

"I love you."

"I love you too. Drive safe."

He kisses me one more time and steps back. "Lock up before I leave."

"So protective," I tease.

"When it comes to my heart, you're damn right I am."

"You make mine beat faster."

"Good. I hope that I always do."

"Me too, handsome. Love you." I push open the door and close it. I've been here before. We both hate leaving the other at the end of the night, and we're notorious for stalling. I turn the lock and then rush to the window to watch him step off the porch and climb back into his truck. I don't step away until I can no longer see his headlights. Today was unexpected and incredible and one I will never forget.

Chapter 7

ORRIN

THIS WEEK HAS BEEN LONG and lonely. I worked late every damn night, including tonight. One of my guys came down with the flu and put us short-handed. I like to meet the deadlines that I give my customers, so I had to do what any business owner does. I had to put in the extra hours to meet deadlines. I'm dead on my feet, and I miss my girl. She brought me dinner to the shop every single night even when I told her she didn't have to but insisted that she wanted to, and it only made me love her more. She wanted to spend that time with me, even though it was only long enough for me to scarf down my food and steal a few kisses.

My last customer just picked up their truck, and they're barely out of the parking lot before I'm hitting the lights, locking the doors, and racing to my truck. Last weekend when I told Jade that her weekend was mine, I didn't know what kind of hell my week was going to be. Now, I can't get home fast enough. She's spending the entire weekend at my place. I want a shower, food, my girl in my arms, and a good night's sleep in that order.

When I pull into my driveway, I could weep when I see Jade's car parked outside of the garage. She's sitting on the front porch. She's in the swing, reading her e-reader. The truck is barely in Park before I'm tearing open the door and rushing up the steps. She's standing when I reach her, so I can easily lift her into my arms and hug the shit out of her. She wraps her legs around my waist and her arms around my neck.

"I missed you too." She chuckles.

"You're staying, right? I need time with you. I missed you more than I thought possible."

"Yeah, I'm staying. I made dinner." She points to the Crock-Pot sitting by the front door. "I put a roast on with potatoes and carrots before I left for work this morning. I assumed it would be another late night for you."

"That sounds perfect. Come on, let's get inside, close the blinds, and lock the doors."

She laughs. "That's a little excessive, don't you think?"

"Nope." I unlock the door and pick up the Crock-Pot, stepping back and giving her room to enter with her bag. "That's the best fucking thing I've seen all week," I say, nodding toward her overnight bag.

"Way to make a girl feel special," she teases.

"That bag belongs to you, baby. Not much more special than that. We're not leaving this house until Sunday night when I know you'll insist you need to go home."

"You never know what the weekend might hold," she tells me with a smile.

"I know that I'm going to hold you." I lean in for a kiss. "Do I need to plug this in?"

"No, it should be plenty warm."

"Let's eat, then we shower."

"You saying I'm dirty?" She raises her eyebrows, her smile barely contained.

"I'm saying I'm dirty, but I don't want to be away from you. Be prepared for me to be attached to you for the next forty-eight hours. Minimum."

"Such a hardship. I guess I can deal."

I tickle her side, and she giggles, stepping out of my reach. "Eat, hungry man."

"I'm hungry, sweetheart, but it's not for dinner." I don't give her time to protest. I plug the Crock-Pot back in, set it on warm, and lift her over my shoulder.

"Orrin!" she screeches. "What are you doing?" A playful swat lands on my ass.

I don't answer her. Instead, I carry her into my bedroom and into the bathroom. I place her ass on the counter. While her face is red from being upside down, her smile is radiant, and her eyes are so full of love, and are pointed at me.

"Sweetheart, I'm going to need to be naked."

"Is this the little bit faster?" She bats her lashes at me.

"Damn right. Strip." I pull my shirt over my head and toss it on the floor. Jade slides off the counter and begins to undress, letting her clothes fall with mine. Why that's sexy to me, I have no idea. It's a pile of clothes. Sure, her black lacey bra is on top of the pile, but it's more than that. It's the simple fact that her things are combined with mine.

This is a glimpse of our future, and I'm here for it.

She's never stayed over. I've asked her several times, but we've kept that line, but it's blurry. No, fuck that. The line is gone. She's mine. I'm hers, and this is happening. At least, I hope that it is.

"You want this?" I ask, reaching in to turn on the shower head.

"I want you."

"You have me, Jade. But I need to hear you say it. I'm missing you, and this won't be what I'd hoped for our first time. Maybe I should just shower quickly and meet you in the bedroom?"

"No. Stop. Orrin, I want you like this. I'll always remember that our first time together was in a shower because you couldn't bear to wait any longer. It's sexy, the way you're looking at me. The way that you want me. I don't need the hearts and flowers. I don't need easy. I just need you."

I want to drop to my knees and beg her to give me her forever. Instead, I take her hand and step into the shower. I help her in after me and pull the door closed. My hand slides behind her neck, and I guide her lips to mine. Her palms land on my chest as she steps closer, which causes her bare breasts to press against my chest, and my hard cock to poke her in the stomach.

She reaches between us and strokes me.

"Hold that thought, sweetheart." I step out of the shower and pull the drawer open in the bathroom. I dig around looking for a condom but can't find one. I open the next drawer, and still nothing. "Shit," I curse.

"What's wrong?" Jade asks.

I look over to find the shower door still open and my girl with her head tilted back, letting the water wash over her while her eyes are on me. My cock weeps, my heart hammers in my chest, and my aggravation builds.

"Condom," I choke out. "I meant to grab some this week and forgot, and I don't have any. I... fuck." I run my hands through my wet hair.

She smiles. "First of all, grab a towel. You're dripping all over the floor. Second, I picked up a box. I wasn't sure if you had any, and I know it's been a tough week for you, and figured we would use them eventually."

"I fucking love you."

She shakes her head and smiles. "In my bag. I left it in the living room."

I point at her. "Don't move."

"I'll be right here," she assures me.

Forgoing the towel, I make a mad dash to the living room, finding her bag. I grab it and haul ass back to my bedroom. "Jade!" I call out, rushing back into the bathroom. "Where are they?" I ask her.

"Right on top."

I unzip the bag and find the box easily. Not wanting to set her bag on the wet floor, I take it back to my room and place it in the bottom of my closet, all while tearing open the box. I grab a small foil packet and toss the rest of the box on the bed.

By the time I'm back in the bathroom, my cock is covered. I step into the shower, and Jade closes the door behind me. Snaking an arm around her waist, I slip my fingers inside her, wasting no time. "You're ready for me." She moans, and her hands reach out for me, her nails digging into my skin.

"I've been ready for you for weeks," she says cheekily, placing a kiss on my shoulder.

"I thought your insistence that you go home or that I come home meant you weren't ready."

She shrugs. "I wanted to give us time, but I'm done with that. I need you. I don't need the foreplay, not this time. I just need you inside me."

I grip her waist as I drop a kiss on her lips. "Legs around me," I command, sliding my hands to the backs of her thighs as I lift her into my arms. "You sure this is what you want?"

"Orrin, I know why you're asking. You're a good man. You're my man, and that means I'm yours. Trust that if there is something I don't like, I'll tell you. You also need to trust that if you don't fix this ache, I'm going to have to take matters into my own hands."

"While the idea of you doing—" I swallow hard. "—that is sexy as fuck, that's not how this is going to go. Don't worry. We're going to circle back to that," I assure her.

Over the chitchat, I press her back against the wall and reach between us, placing my cock at her entrance. We both moan as I slowly push inside her for the first time. "Fuck." I'm not going to last. I'm about to be a two-pump chump with the woman I love for our first time, and there is nothing I can do about it. "Baby, this is... you're just... damn, you're hot and tight, and I'm ready to come," I ramble.

"Yes, that. Let's do that," she says, resting her head back against the shower wall.

I pull out and push back in, over and over. I'm relentless in the pursuit of our pleasure. I can feel her pussy start to pulse around my cock, and I know she's close. I need her there. I don't know how much longer I'll last. I slow my pace and slide my hand between us. I massage her clit, one, two, three swipes, and she fires off like a rocket.

"Orrin!" She calls out my name, and there is no hope for me. I explode inside her, spilling into the condom. My body shakes with pleasure coming down from the most intense orgasm of my life.

I step away from the cold wall and place her back under the hot spray as I bury my face in her neck. I need to take care of the condom, but damn, I never want to pull out. I just want to live with my cock buried inside of her.

WILLOW RIVER, GA

Eventually, I place her on her feet and make sure she's steady before removing the condom, pulling open the shower door, and tossing it in the trash can. I help Jade shower, making sure to wash every inch of her body. I take great pleasure in roaming my hands over every inch of her.

Once I've finished, I kiss her soundly, before she steps out leaving me to quickly wash off as well. By the time I shut off the water, it's turning cold. Pulling open the shower door, I notice that Jade has already cleaned up our dirty clothes and the pile of water I left on the floor. My girl is standing in front of the mirror watching me. She's wearing a pair of pink and black pajama pants and a blank tank top, sans bra. Her hair is wrapped up in a towel on the top of her head, and without a doubt, she's never been more beautiful to me. My heart rate spikes just looking at her.

"You're beautiful." The words roll across my tongue, spilling my thoughts.

She smiles. "I love you too."

Stepping out, I grab a towel to dry off. While I'm getting dressed while she brushes out her hair. It's very much a scene of domesticity, and I couldn't be happier. Once we're both finished, we head back to the kitchen to have dinner. Jade sits on my lap while we eat because I'm not ready to let her go. I don't think that I ever will be. With our bellies full, we fall into bed exhausted, sated, and happier than

I've ever been. Sleeping with her in my arms is my new favorite pastime. Without a doubt in my mind, I know that I'm holding my future. I can't wait to build a life with her.

"Night," I say, kissing her shoulder.

"Goodnight." The room is quiet other than the sound of our even deep breaths. I'm just about to sleep when she asks, "You sure you want me to stay all weekend

"Sweetheart, I want you to stay always."

Forever.

Thank YOU

for taking the time to read *Stay Always*.

Want more from the Kincaid Brothers?
Pre-order *Stay Over*.
Stay Over is Brooks Kincaid's story

kayleeryan.com/books/stay-over/

Available September 13, 2022

Want to read Deacon and Ramsey's story?
Grab *Never with Me* here:

kayleeryan.com/books/never-with-me/

Never miss a new release:
Newsletter Sign-up

Be the first to hear about free content, new
releases, cover reveals, sales, and more.
kayleeryan.com/subscribe/

Keep Reading for a sneak peek at
Stay Over and *Never with Me*

Stay OVER

Chapter 1

BROOKS

I'M STANDING IN THE BACK of the room, watching as my little cousin smiles up at her future husband. I admit that Deacon and Ramsey together is not something I would have predicted. He's ten years older than her. The same age as Orrin, and Ramsey, she lands in the middle of Archer and Ryder. I never saw it coming, but to see the two of them together, no one questions the love they have for each another.

The crowd, and by the crowd, I mean most of my brothers, chant for them to kiss as they stare lovingly into one another's eyes. Deacon wraps his arms around her, pulling her into his chest, and drops his lips to hers. The moment is so intimate I have to look away, feeling as though I need to give them privacy.

My eyes land on Palmer, and the smile that lights up her face as she watches her brother and her best friend kiss can only be described as pure joy. She radiates happiness for them, and I'm sure there's a little bit of pride there as well. She's the one who got them together, and I've heard her boast about it many times. Even though she brags about setting all of this in motion, she can't hide her happiness for the couple.

"When I get married, I'm not doing any of this engagement party shit," Maverick, one of the twins and the babies in the family, says, stepping up beside me.

I huff out a laugh. "Trust me, my man, when you feel like that"—I point to where Deacon stands with his arm around Ramsey's waist, holding her close to him while they talk to his parents—"about someone, there likely isn't much you wouldn't agree to."

"How would you know?" my little brother challenges.

He and his twin, Merrick, just turned nineteen, and they have so much to learn. "Call it a hunch," I tell him.

He's quiet for a few minutes, and when he speaks again, his words surprise me. "You ever been in love, Brooks?" His voice is softer than it was previously.

"Love like that?" I point to our cousin and her fiancé. "No. There has never been anyone to hold my interest long enough." It's true. I've dated here and there but never anything or anyone serious. Not because I'm against the act of falling ass over heels in love. It's the opposite, in fact. I grew up watching my parents and the love they have for one another. I'll never settle for anything less than what they have.

"Dad's always preaching about working hard and loving harder, yet all of us are still single. I mean, Merrick and me, we're the babies, but the rest of you, well, except for Orrin, are still single."

"Love takes time, kid," I tell him.

I feel a slight punch to my arm and grin. He and Merrick both hate it when we call them kids. "It took Orrin thirty-two years to find the one, and Deacon too. They're the same age. But they found it. We will too. Besides, you're too young to be thinking about settling down."

"I'm not. Not really. I just... you know, these

things make you think, and the way Orrin fell so fast for Jade, I was just curious if it would be like that for the rest of us."

"Honestly, I don't know. I think that sometimes it's fast and others it's like a slow build. There is no timeline you have to follow."

"Yeah," he agrees as Rushton, the middle brother of the nine, joins us.

"What are you two talking about all serious?" His eyes bounce from me to Maverick.

"Mav was just telling me that when he gets married, he's omitting the engagement party," I tell him.

Rushton nods. "You might be on to something, little brother."

After draining the last of my beer, I hold up the empty bottle. "I'm grabbing another. You want one?" I ask Rushton.

"Nah, I'm set." Rushton holds up his bottle of beer.

"I'd love one. Thanks for asking," Maverick quips.

"Yeah, not happening. Mom would hang me up by my toes." Mav grumbles, making me smile, as I turn away from them and make my way to the bar. If we were at my place or one of the others, I'd let him drink, but this is a different setting, and like I said, Mom would be pissed, and if there is anything that me and my brothers hate, it's when our momma is pissed at us. All nine of us are Momma's boys and damn proud of it.

Reaching the bar, I raise my bottle at the bartender before setting the empty on the bar. I'm just about ready to turn around and do some more people-watching when I feel a shoulder bump into mine. Turning, I see Palmer standing next to me.

"I do good work, huh?" She smiles up at me. Her emerald eyes are sparkling.

"Are you ever going to let them live that down?" I ask her, nodding at the bartender, who places a fresh ice-cold bottle in front of me. "What are you drinking?" I ask her.

"Oh, a beer is fine." She smiles kindly at the bartender, and the woman actually blushes. Palmer turns her attention back to me. "And no, probably not. I have to keep it up so that I have a good case for them to name their firstborn after me."

"I don't know if the world can handle more than one Palmer Setty," I tease.

"Hey, I won't be Setty for long," she fires back.

"Really? I didn't know you were seeing anyone." I take a pull of my beer as the bartender places Palmer's in front of her and quickly scurries away.

"Oh, I'm not. However, I know I don't want to be some spinster cat lady. I believe that there's someone out there for all of us. I just haven't found mine yet."

I hold my beer up, and she taps hers to mine. "Maybe Ramsey needs to get involved, so you don't hold this over her head forever."

"Oh, I'm so going to regardless." Palmer laughs. "She's my best friend, and she's marrying my brother. I set them up. That's lifetime bragging rights, my friend."

"Good to know. I guess my brothers and I can take credit for Orrin and Jade since we all helped him get ready for their first date."

"That gives you like a year, maybe. I mean, I set them up, I planned it, and now they're getting married. Lifetime." She grins, bumping her shoulder into mine once again.

"Savage. I like it."

She nods before turning to face the crowd, resting her back against the bar. I mimic her stance and survey the room.

"Orrin and Jade seem happy." She nods to where my oldest brother has his girlfriend, Jade, wrapped in his arms, swaying back and forth on the dance floor.

"Yeah. Things are getting serious, I think. At

least they are for him." I realize that Jade is one of Palmer's good friends and is her sister Piper's best friend, and I might be freely giving information that I should be keeping to myself.

"No, for her too. She's really into him."

"Good." I nod even though I'm not sure she's looking at me.

"We're probably going to find ourselves at one of these with those two as the guests of honor sooner rather than later."

"You're probably right. My momma will be thrilled. Two weddings and the chance at more grandkids. Declan moved to the top as her favorite when Blakely was born."

"Stop." I turn to look at her to find her smiling up at me. "Your momma is too damn sweet to have favorites."

"Oh, that's not true. Blakely is by far her favorite."

"Am I sensing some jealousy from you?"

"Nah, she's cute as hell. Besides, when she was born, it kept Mom from asking the rest of us when we were going to give her grandchildren. Now that Orrin is in a serious relationship, it's only a matter of time before she starts asking again. Hell, she might already be."

"Carol would never." She places her hand that's

not holding her beer over her heart and acts offended on my mom's behalf.

"Oh, she would. In fact, let's place a bet."

"I thought you left the betting to your brothers," she teases.

"We do, but this calls for one anyway."

"All right, big man. What are the terms?"

"If I win, you have to... you have to be my dance partner for the rest of the night." I don't know where that came from, but I can't take it back. Besides, Palmer is beautiful, and she looks sexy as hell in her little black dress. I could think of worse ways to spend the rest of my cousin's engagement party.

"And if I win, you have to come to my shop and help me put together a new bookshelf I bought for the lobby to display framed photos and store albums of my work. The one I had was too small."

"Done." I hold my hand out for her to shake. She slides her much smaller hand into mine, and a zap of something I can't name hits me out of nowhere. I quickly drop her hand and search the crowd for my brother, pretending that touching her soft skin didn't feel as though I was being electrocuted in the best way.

"Moment of truth," I tell her, nodding to where Orrin and Jade are standing on the opposite side of the room, still swaying back and forth in each other's arms.

"Let's do this." She grabs my hand, and that feeling hits me once again. This time she stops and stares up at me and back to our joined hands before shaking her head and pulling me across the room to my brother and her friend. "Hey, guys," she greets them, dropping my hand.

"What are you up to?" Jade chuckles.

"Who me?" Palmer places her hand against her heart just as she did earlier, feigning innocence.

"Yes, you." Jade smiles at her.

"Well, we"—Palmer looks over and points at me before turning back to Jade and Orrin—"have a little wager going, and the two of you hold the answer."

"This should be good," Orrin chimes in.

"I bet her that Mom has already been asking you when you're going to give her more grandchildren now that you two are getting serious," I tell them.

"Oddly enough, she hasn't mentioned it," Orrin confesses.

"Hah! I win!" Palmer wiggles her hips in that tight-ass dress of hers, and my cock twitches in my jeans.

"Well, not exactly," Jade speaks up.

"Please tell me my mother isn't harassing you about grandkids." Orrin's tone is pleading. His eyes are closed, and his head is tilted back as if he needs the gods of patience to rain down on him.

"Well, she's not harassing me. However, she did mention it last week at Sunday dinner."

"Damn, I missed it." I'm a registered nurse by trade, and I work at the Willow River General Hospital Emergency Department. My hours change in varying stages of twelve-hour shifts, and that includes working every third weekend.

"I'm sorry," Orrin says sincerely. "I'll talk to her."

"No. Don't tell her I told you. She was really sweet about it, and it didn't bother me."

"So we both win." I grin over at Palmer.

She shrugs. "As long as I get my shelf put together, I'm good."

"What did you win?" Jade asks me.

"This one"—I point at Palmer—"has to be my dance partner the rest of the night. I've been avoiding your cousin Jackie all night, and Palmer is my excuse to keep doing so."

"She's... a lot to take on," Jade agrees. "She means well, but she has zero subtlety."

"Subtlety? Is that what you call her grabbing my ass and telling me I owe her a dance?" I ask.

Jade, Palmer, and Orrin all crack up laughing at my expense. "Laugh it up, assholes. I'm telling you, those talon nails of hers bit into the skin even through my jeans."

"Prove it," Palmer challenges, and if I knew it wouldn't send my cousin or my mother into orbit, I'd pull my pants down now to show her.

"How did she get an invite anyway?" I ask them.

"Is that a serious question?" Orrin asks. "Deacon invited what seems like all of Willow River. He's shouting from the rooftops that Ramsey agreed to marry him."

"She's changed him," Palmer says. I turn to look at her, and she has a soft smile on her lips as she watches Deacon and Ramsey where they're talking to Mayor Hanson.

"Damn, he really did invite the entire town." I laugh.

"Well, I guess I have a debt to pay. You think you can manage taking me for a spin out there?" Palmer indicates to the dance floor behind us.

I drain my beer and set it on a nearby table. Palmer takes a hefty drink of hers and then hands the bottle to Jade. "Finish this for me, will you? Hot beer tastes like cat piss." As soon as Jade takes the bottle, Palmer finds my hand and leads me to the dance floor.

She stops and turns to face me, and the song turns slow. Sliding my arm around her waist, I pull her close and begin to sway.

"You're not half bad at this," she says, peering up at me under long lashes. Her hands that have been resting on my chest move to wrap around the back of my neck. The action causes her tits to press tight against me, and I have to make a conscious effort to keep my hardening cock from pressing into her belly.

"Not half bad?" I scoff. "I could dance circles around everyone on this dance floor," I announce with confidence.

"You're going to have to wait until another night for that, big guy." She runs her fingers through the back of my hair. "I'm in the middle of paying my debt."

"Are you saying you can't hang?"

"Oh, I can hang, but these heels are killing my feet."

"Take them off."

"What?"

"You said that the heels were killing your feet, so take them off."

"The floor is probably dirty and sticky, and just no."

"Good call. We can sit," I tell her. "I don't want you hurting yourself just to fulfill a silly bet."

"I'm good, Brooks. Just don't expect me to go dancing circles around everyone here." She winks, and I feel the action in my chest, a tightening that I've never felt before.

I chalk the feeling up to my dry spell. I've been picking up a lot of hours the last few weeks to cover for another nurse who was on maternity leave. That hasn't left much social time. I need to do something about that. I make a mental note to call a few of my brothers so we can hit the town. Maybe head over to Harris and hit a bar there for the night.

"Let me know if you need a break," I tell her.

"Trust me. I will." We're both quiet for a few minutes, just swaying to the slow beat, when her eyes connect with mine. "You know, you could be missing out on a lot of fun by not giving Jackie that dance." She nods behind me, a grin plastered on her face. I twirl us around so I can see what she's talking about.

I have to bite down on my cheek to keep my laughter contained and not draw attention to us or the situation. Jackie is standing between my two baby brothers, and they're all three grinding on each other like they're at a strip club and not the small manor on the outskirts of town.

HOME OF THE KINCAID BROTHERS

"They better hope our momma doesn't see them," I say for Palmer's ears only.

"They're young, and a hot older woman is showing them attention. Let them live it up."

"I'm not breaking that up. I'm not going anywhere near that clusterfuck, but they better hope that Mom doesn't see it. She'll drag them both away by their ears."

"There is so much to be learned from Momma Kincaid." She laughs. "I can only imagine the chaos of raising nine rowdy boys in one house."

"It was all kinds of loud, but it was also fun. My parents let us be kids, and honestly, I'm not sure how we didn't drive them batshit crazy."

"Love."

"What?"

"Love. That's why you didn't drive them batshit crazy."

"You're probably right," I agree. My parents have a love for one another that surpasses anything I've ever witnessed before. And that love they have for each other spilled over to all of us kids. There was never a day growing up that I didn't know that my brothers and I were the most important people in their world. That's how it should be and why I'm still single at the age of twenty-nine. Sure, that's not old by any standards, but I'm also not getting any younger. One day I'll find her. I'll find the woman who tilts my world on its axis and makes me feel whole at the same time. When I do, I'm never letting her go.

Never With Me

PROLOGUE

RAMSEY

I blink hard.

Once.

Twice.

Three times.

I refuse to let the tears fall. Not this time.

I stare at the bruises that surround my wrist. It's easy to make out the fingerprints. I'd show them to my father, but I know it won't matter. He's created the same type of bruise multiple times. Besides, he's just told me that I'm to marry the man responsible for my new markings.

My father doesn't care that the man hurts me or that he has a different woman warm his bed every night. All he cares about is binding our families together. He doesn't care about what I want. He never has. I've spent my life living under his thumb.

I can't take it anymore.

For the first time in my life, I'm going to defy him. I'm scared of the repercussion of doing so, but I'm even more scared to spend my life married to a monster.

"No." My voice is flat and void of any emotion. I learned a long time ago that showing him anything other than obediance isn't tolerated. I don't let him see that his demand has cut me to the quick and that my heart will be forever broken from the man who was supposed to love me unconditionally. Protect me.

"What did you just say?" Anger ramps up in his voice.

Slowly, I lift my head and stare my father in the eye. "I said no."

His nostrils flare, and if it were possible, he'd have smoke coming out of his ears. In all of my twenty years of my life, I've never uttered the word *no* to the man until just now. The look on his face and the way he's clenching and unclenching his fists tells me he's not the least bit impressed. Not that I expected him to be.

My entire life, he's dictated my every move. What I wear, who I'm friends with, and who I date. Currently, it's Robert Barrington, the third, my current boyfriend, and son of my father's business partner. We've been dating since high school, if you want to call it that. Robert does what he wants and keeps me around for when he needs to put on a show. I'm well aware that he's cheated on me multiple times. In fact, it's a daily occurrence. It doesn't bother me. In fact, it's a relief that he's finding it somewhere else.

"You will do as I say," my father spits.

"No." I'm calm on the outside, but my insides are shaking. Rage appears in his eyes, his voice, and he scares me. They both do. I glance out of the corner of my eye and see my mother sitting on the wingback chair sipping her wine. I didn't have to see her take them to know that she's also taken anti-anxiety medication that I'm sure she washed down with said wine.

My mother is weak. She bows down to my father like the good little trophy wife she is, and it makes me sick. I've begged her more times than I can count to leave him. We can run away together and live a happy life, but she refuses. She claims she loves him and she's nothing without him. He's brainwashed her, and it breaks my heart, but at this point in my life, I have to learn to stand up for myself. I refuse to become another version of my mother.

I turn my head when she opens her mouth, thinking she's going to defend me, but instead, it quickly closes as she stands and walks out of the room- turning a blind eye as usual. I watch her leave, which is a mistake. That's why I don't see it coming.

My father's open palm as it lands with a loud clap across my cheek.

Pain explodes across my face. He's spouting his hateful words and threats, and it takes everything in me to remain standing. To not let him see how he's tearing me down. After a few moments I come back to the present, and he's still spewing hate.

"You will marry Robert, and that's final."

"No."

He scoffs. "Do this, or you are dead to me." His gray eyes stare me down with nothing but hatred.

I wait for the pain to increase, like a knife buried in my chest, but it never comes. I'm immune to his threats of cutting me off. And his words "being dead to him?" I've heard them since I was little. He's manipulative and cold, and every day I lose a piece of myself living under his control.

I've had enough. I'd rather be dead to him than to keep living this way. "I won't marry him."

"Leave." His voice is low and commanding. "You take nothing with you. Do you understand me, Ramsey? You're dead to me. Leave." He turns and walks to the small bar and pours himself three fingers of whiskey.

I don't bother to beg or plead with him. Instead, I turn and walk out of the room. I know he said not to take anything with me, but for now, I'm taking my cell phone. I walk outside and go to call someone to pick me up, and I realize I have no one to call. All of my friends are linked to my father in some way, and that has me feeling lonelier than I ever could have imagined.

Scrolling through my contacts, searching for someone, anyone who I can reach out to, I stop when I see my aunt Carol's name. Without thinking, I hit Call, and with the second ring, her voice is filling my ears.

"Ramsey, what a pleasant surprise."

"Aunt Carol," I croak. The emotion of what I'm forced to do hits me hard.

"What's happened? Are you okay? Your momma?" Concern laces her voice.

"I-I'm fine. I just need somewhere to go." Shame washes over me. I don't call my aunt enough, and here I am in trouble and leaning on her.

"Come to me. Come to Willow River." There isn't an ounce of hesitation in her voice.

"I don't have a car."

"Where are you?"

"At my parents' place."

"Do you have money for a cab?"

"Yes."

"Go to the airport. There will be a ticket there waiting for you. I'll email you the information."

"Thank you, Aunt Carol."

"Are you safe, Ramsey?" she asks.

"I'm safe," I reply, looking down at the bruises on my wrist. The pounding in my head intensifies as does the ache in my cheek. I bring my fingers to softly touch the skin that feels warm to the touch. Hot tears burn my eyes, but I blink them away. I need to get to the airport.

"Thank goodness. We can talk about the rest when you get here."

"I-I'm sorry... I didn't know who else to call."

"I'm glad you called me, sweet girl. Whatever it is, it's all going to be all right."

A sob breaks free from my chest. Why couldn't I have been her daughter? I was born to the wrong sister.

"Call a cab, sweetie. Get to the airport. I'll be there waiting for you when you land."

"Thank you."

"Don't thank me, Ramsey. That's what family is for."

I manage to utter a goodbye before ending the call to order a cab. I start walking, needing to be as far away from my parents' estate as I can possibly get. Today starts a new chapter of my life. I'm going to live it on my terms.

More from
KAYLEE RYAN

With You Series:

Anywhere with You | More with You

Everything with You

Soul Serenade Series:

Emphatic | Assured

Definite | Insistent

Southern Heart Series:

Southern Pleasure | Southern Desire

Southern Attraction | Southern Devotion

Unexpected Arrivals Series

Unexpected Reality |Unexpected Fight

Unexpected Fall | Unexpected Bond

Unexpected Odds

More from KAYLEE RYAN

Riggins Brothers Series:

Play by Play / Layer by Layer

Piece by Piece / Kiss by Kiss

Touch by Touch | Beat by Beat

Standalone Titles:

Tempting Tatum | Unwrapping Tatum | Levitate

Just Say When | I Just Want You

Reminding Avery

Hey, Whiskey | Pull You Through

Remedy | The Difference

Trust the Push | Forever After All

Misconception | Never with Me

Entangled Hearts Duet:

Agony | Bliss

More from KAYLEE RYAN

Cocky Hero Club:
Lucky Bastard

Mason Creek Series:
Perfect Embrace

Out of Reach Series:
Beyond the Bases | Beyond the Game

Beyond the Play | Beyond the Team

Co-written with Lacey Black:

Fair Lakes Series:
It's Not Over | Just Getting Started

Can't Fight It

More from KAYLEE RYAN

Acknowledgments

To my readers:

Thank you for your continued support. If you've made it this far, you've devoured another one of my books, and I can't tell you what it means to me that you picked my words for your escape. Thank you for choosing Stay Always. I cannot wait for you to meet the rest of the Kincaid brothers!

To my family:

I could not do this without your never-ending support. Thank you for standing beside me while I chase my dreams.

Integrity Formatting:

Thank you for making the paperbacks beautiful. You're amazing, and I cannot thank you enough for all that you do.

Wander Aguiar:

Thank you for an image that brings Orrin and Jade to life. It was a pleasure working with you and your team.

Book Cover Boutique:

You nailed the design on this series. Thank you so much for taking my vision and bringing it to life.

Lacey Black:

I don't really know what I can say that I haven't already said, except I love you, my friend. Thank you for being my constant pillar of support and sounding board. Even when it's not one of our co-writes, you're there to bounce ideas and read scenes, and your friendship is invaluable. Thank you for being amazing.

My beta team:

Jamie, Stacy, Lauren, Erica, and Franci, I would be lost without you. You read my words as much as I do, and I can't tell you what your input and all the time you give means to me. Countless messages and bouncing ideas, you ladies keep me sane with the characters being anything but. Thank you from the bottom of my heart for taking this wild ride with me.

Give Me Books:

With every release, your team works diligently to get my book in the hands of bloggers. I cannot tell you how thankful I am for your services.

Julie Deaton:

Thank you for giving this book a set of fresh final eyes.

Becky Johnson:

I could not do this without you. Thank you for pushing me and making me work for it.

Chasidy Renee:

Thank you for everything you do. How did I survive without you before now? No matter what the task, you're always there with your never-ending support. Thank you so very much for all that you do.

Bloggers:

Thank you, it doesn't seem like enough. You don't get paid to do what you do. It's the kindness of your heart and your love of reading that fuels you. Without you, without your pages, your voice, your reviews, and spreading the word, it would be so much harder, if not impossible, to get my words in the reader's hands. I can't tell you how much your never-ending support means to me. Thank you for being you. Thank you for all that you do.

To my reader group, Kaylee's Crew:

You are my people. I love all of the messages and emails you send me. I love the little book community we've created. You are my family. Thank you for all of your love and support, not just with books but with life. No matter what I decide to write, you are there, ready to consume every word. Thank you for being the amazing group of people that you are.

Much love,

Kaylee Ryan
AUTHOR